Mythical Creatures
PHOENIXES

BY THOMAS KINGSLEY TROUPE

BELLWETHER MEDIA • MINNEAPOLIS, MN

Torque brims with excitement perfect for thrill-seekers of all kinds. Discover daring survival skills, explore uncharted worlds, and marvel at mighty engines and extreme sports. In *Torque* books, anything can happen. Are you ready?

This edition first published in 2021 by Bellwether Media, Inc.

No part of this publication may be reproduced in whole or in part without written permission of the publisher.
For information regarding permission, write to Bellwether Media, Inc., Attention: Permissions Department,
6012 Blue Circle Drive, Minnetonka, MN 55343.

Library of Congress Cataloging-in-Publication Data

Names: Troupe, Thomas Kingsley, author.
Title: Phoenixes / Thomas Kingsley Troupe.
Description: Minneapolis, MN : Bellwether Media, 2021. | Series: Torque | Includes bibliographical references and index. | Audience: Ages 7-12 | Audience: Grades 4-6 | Summary: "Engaging images accompany information about phoenixes. The combination of high-interest subject matter and light text is intended for students in grades 3 through 7"–Provided by publisher.
Identifiers: LCCN 2020014878 (print) | LCCN 2020014879 (ebook) | ISBN 9781644872765 | ISBN 9781681037394 (ebook)
Subjects: LCSH: Phoenix (Mythical bird)–Juvenile literature.
Classification: LCC GR830.P4 K56 2021 (print) | LCC GR830.P4 (ebook) | DDC 398/.469–dc23
LC record available at https://lccn.loc.gov/2020014878
LC ebook record available at https://lccn.loc.gov/2020014879

Text copyright © 2021 by Bellwether Media, Inc. TORQUE and associated logos are trademarks and/or registered trademarks of Bellwether Media, Inc.

Editor: Rebecca Sabelko   Designer: Josh Brink

Printed in the United States of America, North Mankato, MN.

TABLE OF CONTENTS

THE LEGEND OF THE FIERY BIRD	4
AN ANCIENT BIRD	8
THE FLAMES STILL BURN	18
GLOSSARY	22
TO LEARN MORE	23
INDEX	24

THE LEGEND OF THE FIERY BIRD

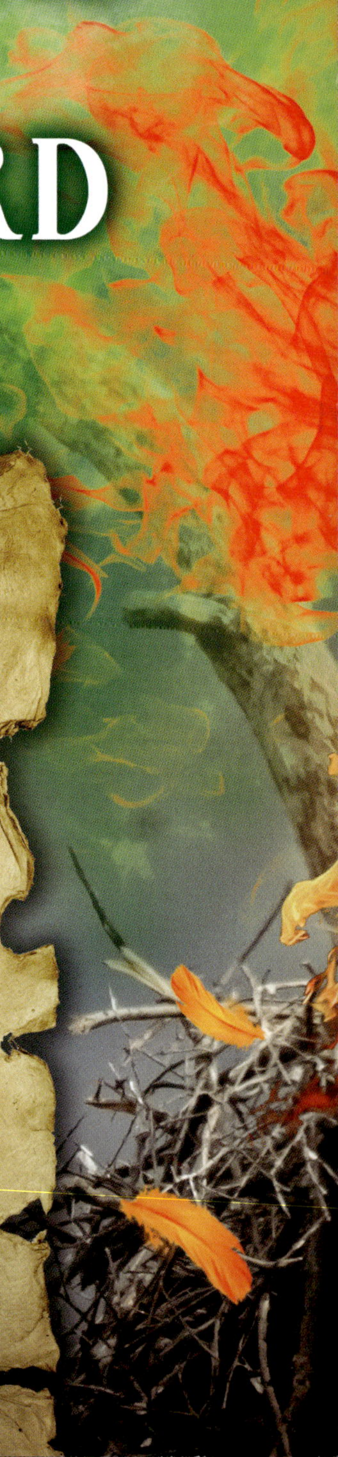

A warm wind whips your face. A flash of color flies past you. A bright phoenix hovers in the sky. Its red and gold feathers shine in the sun.

The 500-year-old bird circles its nest of wood before it lands. The nest suddenly bursts into flames. The bird burns to ash. A moment later, a new phoenix rises!

Super Powers
It is believed people cannot tell a lie around a phoenix. Its tears also hold special healing powers!

According to **legends**, the phoenix is a large, mighty bird. It has bright red, yellow, and purple feathers. The bird can have bright yellow eyes. It may also have blue eyes that shine like jewels. The ancient bird **symbolizes** power. It also stands for **renewal** and **rebirth**.

Only one phoenix can exist at a time. It destroys itself only to be reborn!

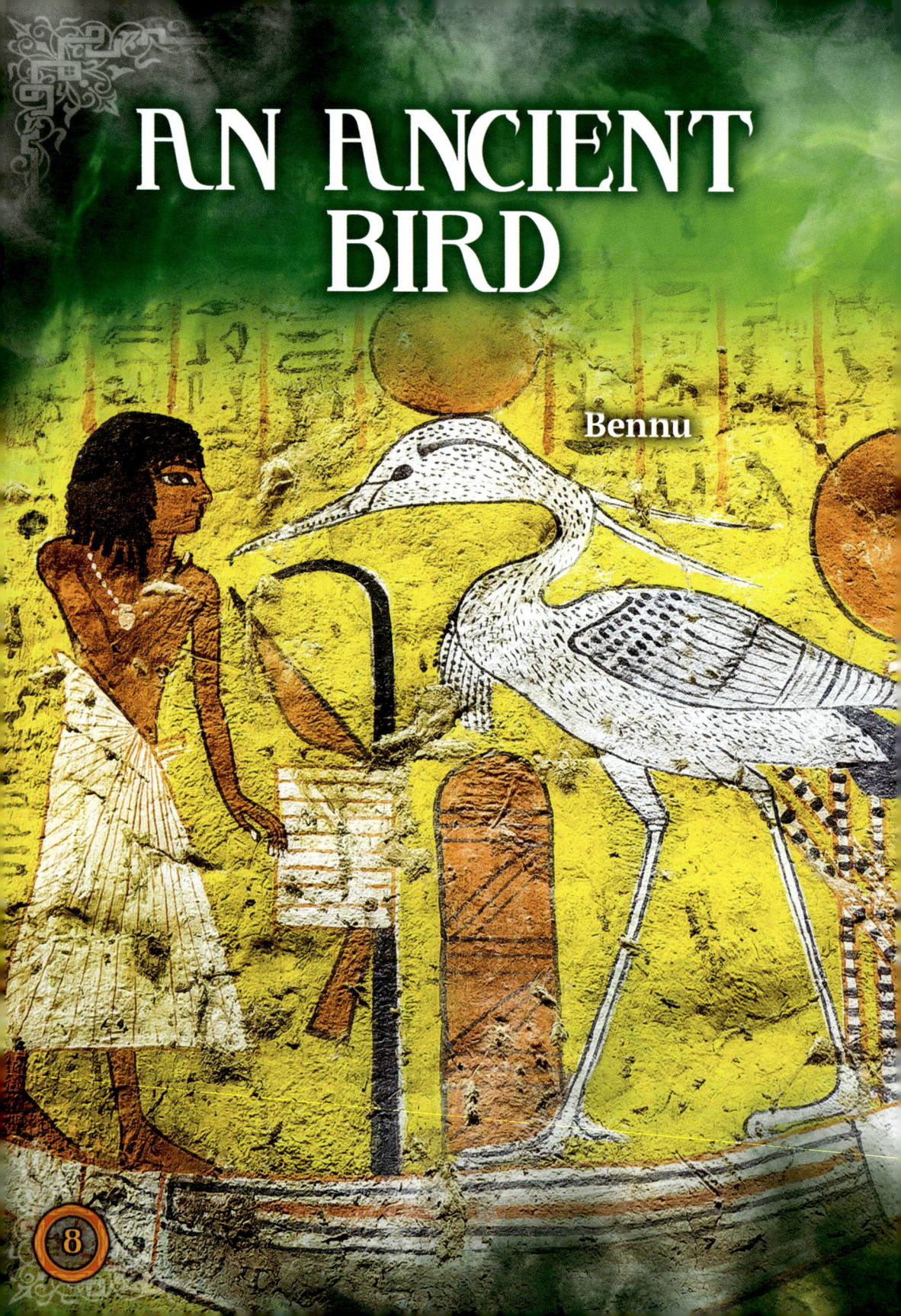

The origins of the phoenix can be traced to ancient Egypt. The Egyptian god Bennu looked a lot like a heron. It had long legs and a long beak.

Bennu was **worshipped** for its connection to the Egyptian creation god Ra. The bird was the soul of Ra. It was also a symbol for the rising and setting sun.

Phoenix Origin

The fenghuang is known as the Chinese phoenix. This colorful bird was first mentioned during the **Shang Dynasty**. It brought **harmony** to the world. Many believed it appeared before the death of an **emperor**.

The fenghuang often wore Chinese symbols that stood for virtue, duty, practice, understanding, and trust. It was believed the bird was a sign of world peace.

Ancient Greek writing also included the phoenix. In the 700s BCE, Hesiod described the long life of the bird. Centuries later, Herodotus retold the Egyptian **myth**. He gave the bird red and gold feathers.

Christians started to use the phoenix as a symbol around 100 CE. The bird's power was linked to Jesus.

Hesiod

Phoenix Myths Around the World

thunderbird
(North America)

the fenghuang
(China)

the roc
(Madagascar)

Simurgh
(Iran)

The phoenix continued to be used as a symbol for hundreds of years. It was popular in art and **literature** during the European **Renaissance**.

Many famous writers used the phoenix to describe special things in life. William Shakespeare linked the bird to love. Ben Jonson used the powerful creature as a warning. The bird showed people that **greed** was foolish.

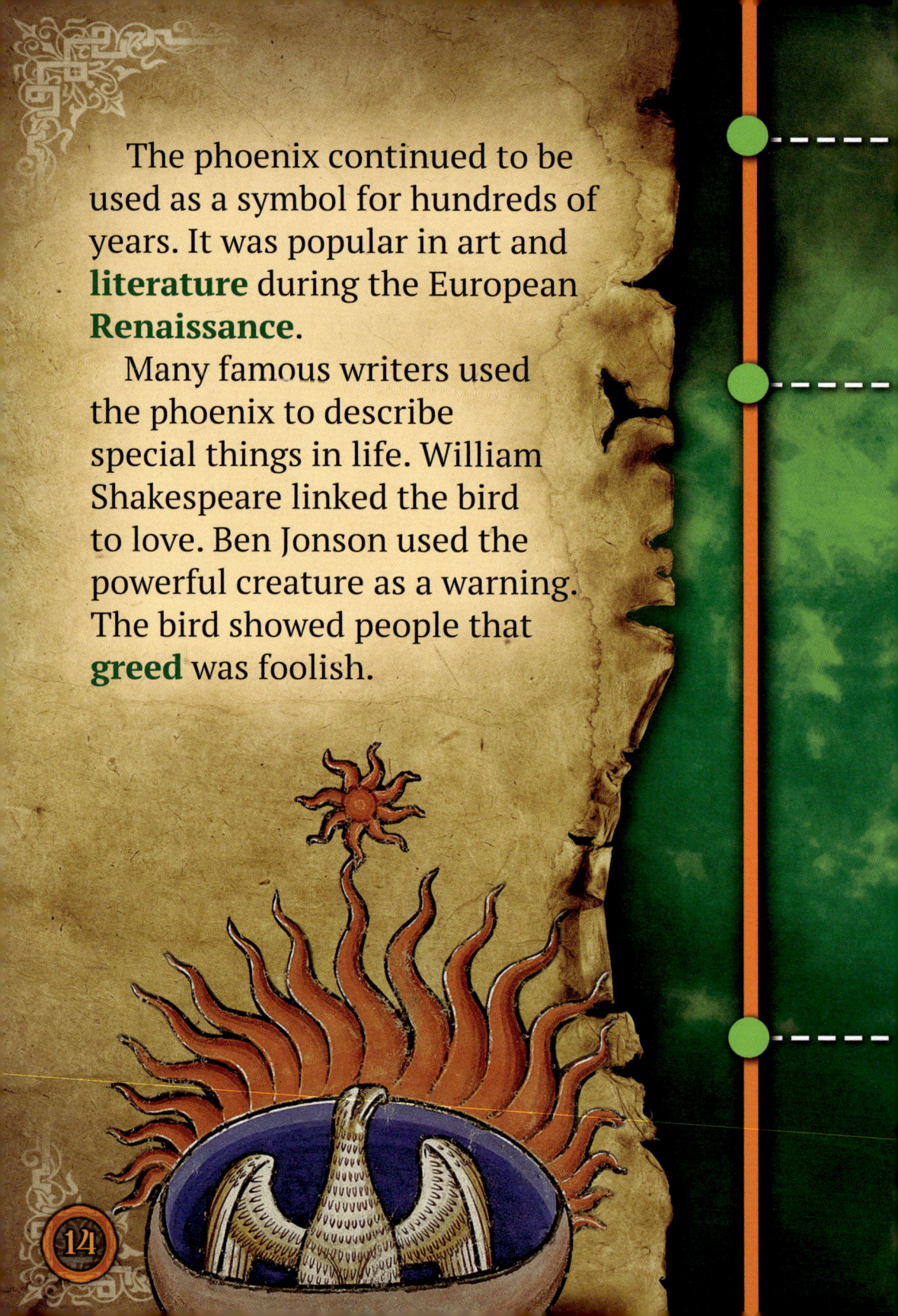

Phoenix Timeline

1760 to 1030 BCE: The fenghuang appears during the Shang Dynasty

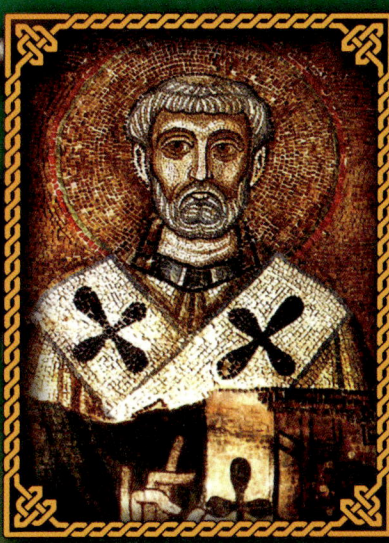

Around 100s CE: Saint Clement describes the phoenix as a symbol in Christianity

1601: William Shakespeare's *The Phoenix and the Turtle* is published

Goliath heron

Many scientists believe the Egyptian god Bennu was **inspired** by a real bird. Ancient Egyptian art shows images of a bright yellow bird. Many scientists think it is a yellow wagtail. But this bird is very small. It weighs less than 1 ounce (28 grams)!

Scientists also believe the idea of the phoenix may have come from herons. **Fossils** of a giant heron were found on the coast of the Red Sea!

yellow wagtail

THE FLAMES STILL BURN

The myth of the phoenix is still around today! But it is rarely shown rising from the ashes of its burning nest. It is most often shown as a flaming bird in flight.

The word "phoenix" is used in the business world. A phoenix company is a company that is created from another company that failed.

Media Mention

Character: Moltres

First Appearances: 1996 video games *Pokémon Red* and *Blue*

Other appearances: *Pokémon Sword and Shield* (2019), *Pokémon Quest* (2018), *Pokémon Ultra Sun* and *Moon* (2017), *Pokémon Go* (2016)

Power: controls fire

The phoenix appears in many movies and books! In the Harry Potter series, Professor Dumbledore kept the mythical bird as a pet. Its name was Fawkes.

The phoenix plays a special role as a magical creature. Interest in this fiery bird is reborn year after year!

Fawkes

Phoenix spacecraft

Space Phoenix

In 2008, a spacecraft named *Phoenix* landed on Mars to study the red planet.

GLOSSARY

emperor—a male ruler of a group of countries or states; emperors once ruled China.

fossils—the remains of living things that lived long ago

greed—a selfish desire to have more of something

harmony—peace and calm

inspired—to cause something to happen or to be created

legends—stories from the past that are believed by many people but cannot be proved to be true

literature—written works, often books, that are highly respected

myth—an ancient story about the beliefs or history of a group of people; myths also try to explain events.

rebirth—new life or being born again

Renaissance—a period of European history from the 1300s to the 1600s when there was interest in science, art, and literature

renewal—the act of making something new, fresh, or strong again

Shang Dynasty—a period of Chinese rule from around 1760 to 1030 BCE

symbolizes—stands for something else

worshipped—honored or respected as a god

TO LEARN MORE

AT THE LIBRARY

Cotton, Jacqueline S. *Phoenix*. New York, N.Y.: AV2 by Weigl, 2018.

Lawrence, Sandra, and Stuart Hill. *The Atlas of Monsters: Mythical Creatures from Around the World*. Philadelphia, Pa.: Running Press Kids, 2019.

Mills, Andrea. *Mythical Beasts*. New York, N.Y.: DK Publishing, 2018.

ON THE WEB

Factsurfer.com gives you a safe, fun way to find more information.

1. Go to www.factsurfer.com

2. Enter "phoenixes" into the search box and click 🔍.

3. Select your book cover to see a list of related content.

INDEX

appearance, 4, 7, 9, 10, 12, 17

around the world, 13

art, 14, 17

Bennu, 8, 9, 17

business, 18

Christians, 12

Egypt, 9, 12, 17, 19

explanations, 17

fenghuang, 10, 11

flames, 4, 18

fossils, 17

Harry Potter (series), 20

Herodotus, 12

heron, 9, 16, 17

Hesiod, 12

history, 9, 10, 12, 14

Jesus, 12

Jonson, Ben, 14

legends, 7

literature, 14

Moltres, 20

myth, 12, 13, 18

nest, 4, 18

origins, 9

Phoenix (spacecraft), 21

Phoenix, Arizona, 19

powers, 6, 7, 12

Ra, 9

rebirth, 7, 20

Renaissance, 14

scientists, 17

Shakespeare, William, 14

Shang Dynasty, 10

symbol, 7, 9, 10, 12, 14

timeline, 14-15

yellow wagtail, 17

The images in this book are reproduced through the courtesy of: Safonov, front cover (hero head); Xcages, front cover (background); Mike Pellinni, front cover (background); Ellerslie, p. 3; Nagel Photography, pp. 4-5; KGrif, pp. 4-5 (background); Mondadori Portfolio/ Getty, pp. 6-7; Science History Images/ Alamy, pp. 7, 13 (bottom right); Alain Guilleux/ Alamy, p. 8; Chronicle/ Alamy, pp. 10, 15 (top); Asar Studios/ Alamy, pp. 10-11; Cola Images/ Alamy, p. 12; Paul Thompson/ Alamy, p. 13 (top left); Olaf Krüger/ Alamy, pp. 13 (bottom left), 18; Godong/ Alamy, p. 13 (top right); Phoenix777/ Wiki Commons, p. 14; Google Cultural Institute/ Wiki Commons, p. 15 (middle); World History Archive/ Alamy, p. 15 (bottom); Charlotte Bleijenberg, pp. 16-17; xpixel, p. 17; funstarts33/ Alamy, pp. 18-19; Danny Ye, p. 20 (top); Anton_Ivanov, p. 20 (bottom); NASA/JPL/Corby Waste/ Wiki Commons, p. 21; Stone36, p. 23; Patrik Ruzic, p. 23 (phoenix).